Hedgehugs

and the
Hattiepillar

Steve Wilson & Lucy Tapper

Henry Holt and Company
NEW YORK

Horace and Hattie are
the very best of friends.

There are so many things
they like to do together.

They like to watch blossoms fall from the trees.

They like to look for the first star of the night.

They like to play hide-and-seek in the meadow.

And on clear nights, they try to catch the moon.

When Horace is busy,
Hattie practices handstands
among the dandelions.

When Hattie is busy,
Horace climbs to the
top of his favorite tree.

One day, Horace and Hattie found

something interesting under a leaf.

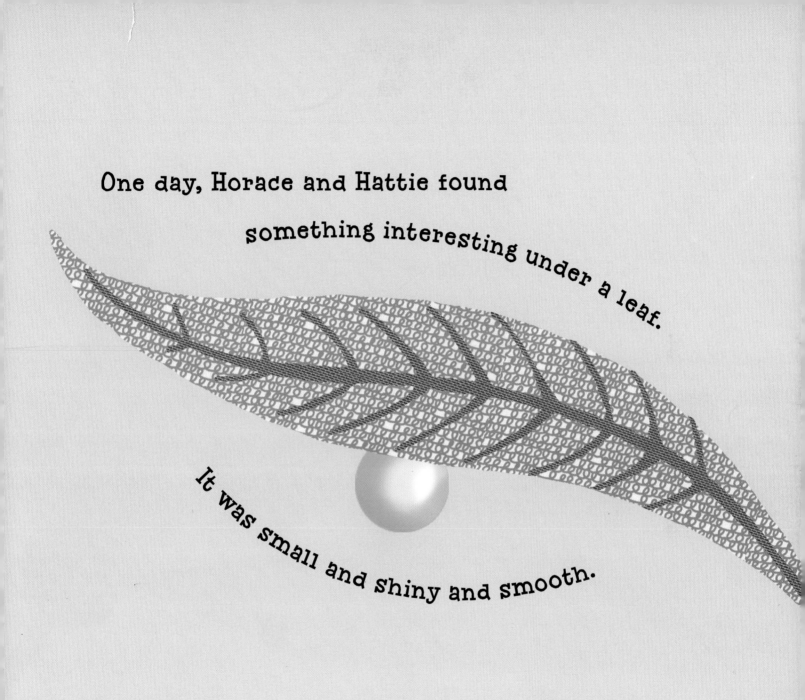

It was small and shiny and smooth.

All of a sudden, out crawled a wriggly, stripy thing!

It looked at Horace and Hattie.

Then it started to eat.

In no time at all, the leaf was gone.

Horace and Hattie found more leaves.

The stripy thing ate and ate. It got bigger and bigger . . .

... and **bigger**

and **bigger!**

Then it stopped.

It made a soft, silky
bed, and there it slept   for many days

and many nights.

One sunny morning,
the little bed opened up.

Out crawled something beautiful,
colorful, and wonderful.

It looked at Horace and Hattie,
waved its wings,

and fluttered away.

This gave Horace an idea.

If they ate a lot and slept in a soft, silky bed, would they turn into something colorful and wonderful too?

Hattie munched.   Horace crunched.

They ate until their tummies were full.

They scooped and gathered and collected flowers until they had a fluffy bed.

Horace and Hattie nestled in the petals
and drifted off to sleep.

When they woke up, Hattie looked at Horace,

and Horace looked at Hattie. Had they changed?

Yes!

They were beautiful, colorful, and wonderful!

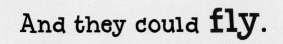

And they could **fly**.

For Doobs & Hobster

x

Henry Holt and Company, LLC, *Publishers since 1866*
175 Fifth Avenue, New York, New York 10010 • mackids.com

Library of Congress Cataloging-in-Publication Data
Names: Wilson, Steve, 1974- author. | Tapper, Lucy, illustrator.
Title: Hedgehugs and the Hattiepillar / Steve Wilson and Lucy Tapper.
Description: First American edition. | New York : Henry Holt and Company,
2016. | "First published in the United Kingdom in 2015 by Maverick Arts
Publishing Ltd"—Title page verso. | Summary: "Horace and Hattie watch a
caterpillar become a butterfly . . . and are inspired to attempt a
transformation of their own!" —Provided by publisher.
Identifiers: LCCN 2015034860 |
ISBN 9781627794145 (hardback) | ISBN 9781627798471 (board book)
Subjects: | CYAC: Hedgehogs—Fiction. | Caterpillars—Fiction. |
Metamorphosis—Fiction. | BISAC: JUVENILE FICTION / Social Issues /
Friendship. | JUVENILE FICTION / Animals / Mice, Hamsters, Guinea Pigs, etc.
Classification: LCC PZ7.1.W58 Hg 2016 | DDC [E]—dc23
LC record available at http://lccn.loc.gov/2015034860

Our books may be purchased in bulk for promotional, educational, or business use.
Please contact your local bookseller or the Macmillan Corporate and Premium Sales Department
at (800) 221-7945 ext. 5442 or by e-mail at MacmillanSpecialMarkets@macmillan.com.

First published in the United Kingdom in 2015 by Maverick Arts Publishing Ltd.
First American edition—2016
Printed in China by RR Donnelley Asia Printing Solutions Ltd., Dongguan City, Guangdong Province

1 3 5 7 9 10 8 6 4 2